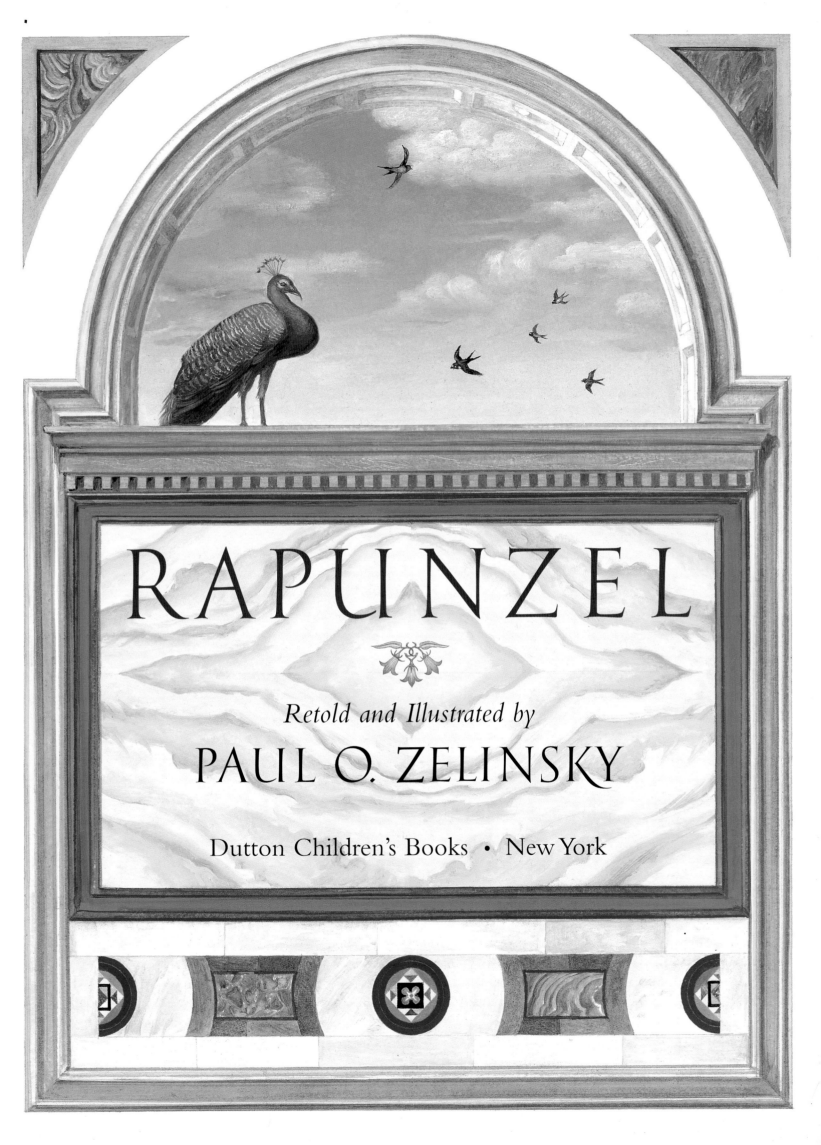

RAPUNZEL

Retold and Illustrated by

PAUL O. ZELINSKY

Dutton Children's Books • New York

Library of Congress Cataloging-in-Publication Data

Zelinsky, Paul O.
Rapunzel/by Paul O. Zelinsky.—1st ed.
p.   cm.
Summary: A retelling of the German folktale in which
a beautiful girl with long golden hair is kept imprisoned
in a lonely tower by a sorceress.
ISBN 0-525-45607-4 (hardcover)
[1. Fairy tales.   2. Folklore—Germany.]   I. Title.
PZ8.Z38Rap   1997   398.2′0943′02—dc21   96-50260   CIP   AC

Published in the United States 1997 by Dutton Children's Books,
a division of Penguin Books USA Inc.
375 Hudson Street, New York, New York 10014

Designed by Amy Berniker and Paul O. Zelinsky
Hand lettering on jacket and title page by John Stevens

Manufactured in China
First Edition
10

I lovingly dedicate this book to my family—
Anna, Rachel, and Deborah

Long ago, there lived a man and a woman who had no children. As year followed year, this was their only sorrow. Then one spring, the wife felt her dress growing tight around her waist. Joyfully she said to her husband, "We are going to have a child at last."

The wife liked to sit by a small window at the back of their house and look down into a beautiful garden. Flowers grew there, and rare fruits and herbs of every kind. The garden belonged to a sorceress, who had enclosed it on all sides with a high wall. No one ever dared to enter it.

One day, as the wife sat by the window, her eyes fixed on a bed of rapunzel. The herb looked so luxuriant, so green and thick and fresh, that she felt a terrible longing to taste it. Day after day her craving grew, until she began to suffer from it. She became pale and wretched, and said to her husband, "If I cannot eat some of the rapunzel from the garden behind our house, I am going to die."

Her husband was alarmed to hear such desperate words. He loved his wife dearly, and saw no choice but to bring her some of the rapunzel.

Ten times, twenty times he circled the garden wall, but found neither door nor gate. So, lowering himself through the window at the back of the house, he climbed down into the sorceress' garden. Quickly he pulled up as much rapunzel as he could hold and scrambled back up through the window.

His wife made a salad of the roots and greens, and devoured it with a wild hunger. So intensely delicious was the taste that she nearly fainted as she ate. Yet the next day her craving for rapunzel was even fiercer than before.

Once again the husband made his way down the wall and into the garden. But this time as he reached for the rapunzel, the sorceress rose up before him. "How dare you come here to steal my rapunzel!" she cried. "Oh, it will serve you ill!"

"Have mercy on me," the man begged. "My wife is carrying our child. She has seen your rapunzel from our window and conceived such a longing for it that she will die unless she can eat some. What am I to do?"

The sorceress considered his words. "If what you say is true, you may take the rapunzel that you need. But in return, you must give me the child your wife will bear."

The frightened husband did not know what to say. Rather than see his wife die, he agreed to the demand. And when the child was born, the sorceress appeared in the room. She named the baby girl Rapunzel and carried her away.

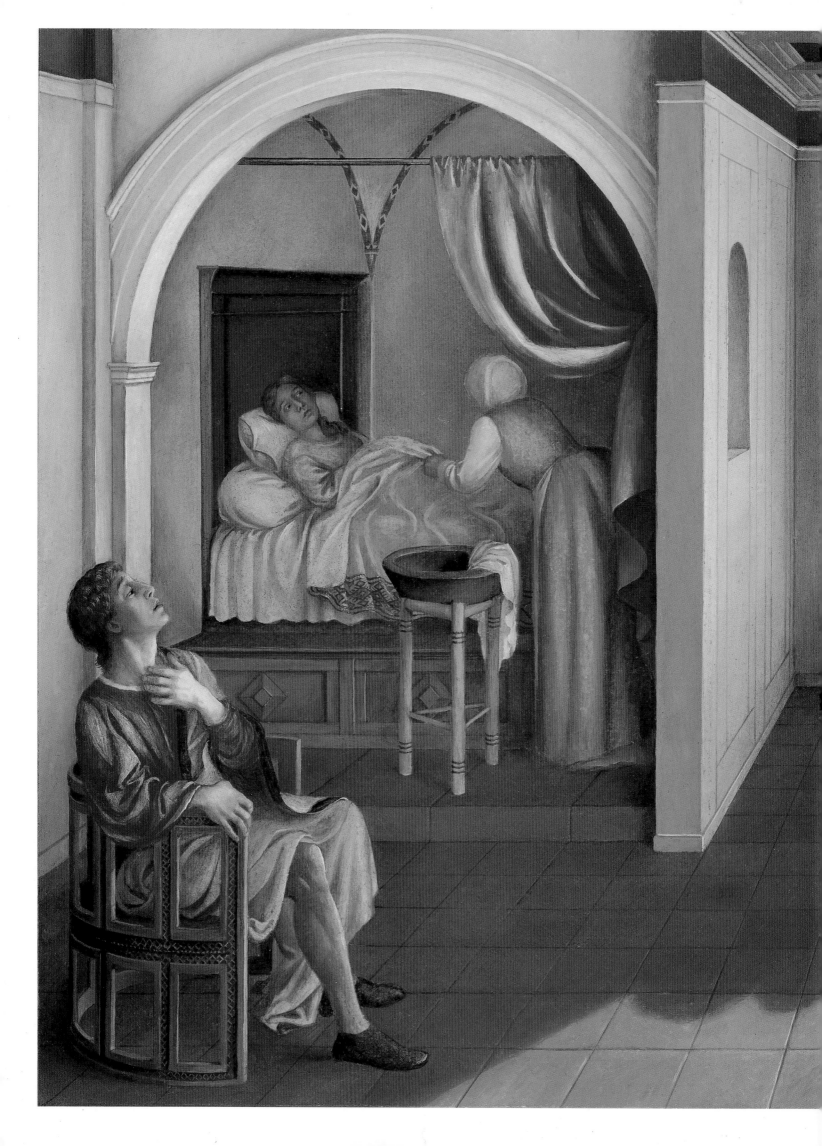

The sorceress cared for the baby, seeing to her every need. Rapunzel grew to be a child of rare beauty, with pale skin and an abundance of flowing red-gold hair. When she reached the age of twelve, the sorceress led her into the forest to live in a high tower.

The tower was a great column rising in the middle of the woods. Although it looked narrow on the outside, on the inside it was large, with many elegant rooms. Yet no door led into this tower, and its only window was at the very top.

When the sorceress wished to enter, she stood below the window and called, "Rapunzel, Rapunzel, let down your hair." Then Rapunzel would unpin her silky braids, wind them around a hook on the window frame, and let them tumble all the way to the ground. The sorceress would grab hold of them and hoist herself up.

For years, Rapunzel lived alone in her rooms above the treetops, visited only by the sorceress. Then one day a king's son came riding through the woods. As he neared the tower, he heard a voice sweeter than any he had ever known. It was Rapunzel, singing to the forest birds. Charmed by her voice, the prince fell deeply in love. He circled the tower ten times, twenty times, but found no entrance. "How strange this tower is," he said to himself, and felt he would die of sadness.

He inquired at the nearest houses, where he was told that the tower belonged to a sorceress, who was keeping a young girl shut away inside. Day after day the prince returned, hoping to glimpse the girl whose sweet singing had moved him so.

One morning he saw the sorceress appear below the window and call up, "Rapunzel, Rapunzel, let down your hair!"

At once the prince knew how he, too, might enter the tower.

The next evening he stood under the window and called, "Rapunzel, Rapunzel, let down your hair!" Rapunzel's hair came billowing down. The king's son took hold of it and pulled himself up.

"Heaven preserve me!" cried Rapunzel when the prince stepped through her window, for she had never set eyes on a man before. But he began to speak to her in such a friendly way that her fear was soon gone.

"Your singing was so beautiful," the prince told her, "that I knew I must see your face, or my heart could have no peace." Rapunzel saw that he was young and handsome; in her own heart she felt a happiness she had never known. And when the prince, grown bold, proposed to marry her then and there, she consented. They held a ceremony in the tower, and every evening after that, he returned. The sorceress, who came only by day, knew nothing of his visits.

One day when the sorceress entered the tower, Rapunzel said, "If you please, Stepmother, help me with my dress. It is growing so tight around my waist, it doesn't want to fit me anymore."

Instantly the sorceress understood what Rapunzel did not. "Oh, you wicked child!" she shrieked. "What do I hear you say? I thought I had kept you safe, away from the whole world, but you have betrayed me!"

In a rage, she seized the braids and coils of Rapunzel's silky hair and sheared them off. Then she sent the miserable girl to a wild country, to live alone with no one to care for her. After some months in this wilderness, Rapunzel gave birth to twins, a boy and a girl.

Once the sorceress had cast Rapunzel out of the tower, she gathered the cutoff hair and fastened it to the window-hook. That evening, when the prince called up, "Rapunzel, Rapunzel, let down your hair!" she let the hair cascade down. The poor prince pulled himself up to the window, only to be confronted by the sorceress, her eyes wild with fury. "So you have come to fetch your dearest darling?" she cried. "Well, you shall not see her again—Rapunzel is lost to you forever!"

Struck through with grief, the prince let go of the braids, and he plummeted to the ground.

Although the fall should have killed him, the prince lived. But his eyes were hurt; he could no longer see. Wretched and blind, he stumbled from place to place, eating nothing but roots and berries, thinking of nothing but the loss of his beloved wife. After a year of wandering in such misery, he came into the same wilderness where Rapunzel was living with her children. There one day he heard a voice so dear to him that he rushed toward it. Rapunzel saw him and opened her arms to him, weeping.

As Rapunzel embraced the prince, two of her tears fell into his eyes. Suddenly his vision grew clear; once again the prince could see.

He gazed at Rapunzel and at their two beautiful children. He looked up at the hills beyond the rocky landscape and knew that he was not lost. The prince led his family out of the wilderness toward his kingdom, where they were received with great joy.

There they lived a long life, happy and content.

A Note About "Rapunzel"

"Rapunzel" has a rich and surprising history. Although Wilhelm and Jacob Grimm included it in their famous collection of German folktales, *Children's and Household Tales*, their "Rapunzel" was hardly the rustic story of "folk" origin that they implied it to be. It was actually their own adaptation of a rather elegant story of the same name, published in Leipzig some twenty years earlier. That "Rapunzel" was a loose German translation of a much older French literary fairy tale, which itself drew heavily on a story published in Naples, a story that did have a local folktale as its source.

Il Pentamerone, or *The Tale of Tales,* written in the Neapolitan dialect by Giambattista Basile and published in 1634, was a colorful and sometimes ribald collection of stories-within-a-framing-story, in the manner of *The Thousand and One Nights.* One of its tales was "Petrosinella."

In this story a pregnant mother, craving her witch-neighbor's parsley (called *petrosine* in Neapolitan), is caught in the act of stealing it. Seven years later the witch collects on her debt, taking the young, long-haired Petrosinella to live with her in a tower. After some time, a prince happens on the tower, climbs the braids hanging from its window, and falls in love with Petrosinella. A neighbor sees his nighttime visits and warns the witch that Petrosinella may soon run away. The witch brags that the girl is held by a charm and cannot flee. But Petrosinella and her prince elope, using a rope and the witch's own amulets: magic acorns that allow them to evade her fierce pursuit.

When a vogue for fairy tales swept Europe in the late seventeenth century, *Il Pentamerone* inspired a French noblewoman, Charlotte-Rose de Caumont La Force, to write her own *Tale of Tales.* Published in 1697, these stories were written in a nunnery—La Force had been banished from Louis XIV's court for her scandalous satirical novels. *La Conte des Contes* included "Persinette," an elaborate tale based in part on "Petrosinella."

Here a newly wed and pregnant young wife urges her husband to steal parsley (*persil*) from the neighboring garden of a fairy. The husband is caught, and the fairy claims the child, Persinette, at birth. Twelve years later the fairy moves the long-haired girl into a magical silver tower deep in the woods. There, in its many glowing rooms, Persinette lives amidst

great luxury; there she is discovered by, and soon married to, the handsome prince. In time, her pregnancy scandalizes the fairy, who cuts the girl's hair, banishes her (to a lovely seaside cottage), and tricks the prince, resulting in his blindness. After a year, when Persinette's tears heal the prince's eyes, the reunited family must still undergo some terrible ordeals—food turning into stone, birds into dragons and harpies—before the fairy takes pity and saves them.

Among the translations of "Persinette," one by Joachim Christoph Friedrich Schulz, in his 1790 *Kleine Romane*, found favor with the German public. Schulz dealt freely with La Force's text (to which he gave no attribution), altering phrases and adding details, such as the tight dress that betrays the girl's pregnancy to the old woman. And for parsley he substituted the altogether unrelated herb called *Rapunzel* in German and, in English, rampion.

(Rampion is both an ornamental flower and a salad green, edible in its leaf and tuberous root, with a flavor somewhere between watercress and arugula. It is not related to the wild onion known as rampion or ramp, a traditional dish in some parts of the United States. In this book I have chosen to refer to the herb only as "rapunzel.")

The Grimms wrote in the appendix to the first edition of their collection (1812) that Schulz's "Rapunzel" was "undoubtedly derived from an oral tale." Apparently they were unaware of its French provenance, though they did mention its similarity to "Petrosinella." For their own version of the tale, they shortened and recast Schulz's story in the harsher style of their other tales. So La Force/Schulz's newlyweds became a couple burdened with infertility; the magical tower turned into a prison tower, in which no marriage ceremony occurred; and Rapunzel's place of exile became an inhospitable wilderness. In the Grimms' first edition, Rapunzel's tight dress gave away her secret trysts, but by the second edition it was her now familiar slip of the tongue: "Why are you so heavy to pull up, while the prince is here in the blink of an eye?"

Although the Grimm brothers purportedly created their collection to preserve ancient stories in a pure state, untouched by literary influence, the history of "Rapunzel" shows how far from this goal the reality actually fell. In recent years, scholars of folklore have traced the confluence of oral traditions and literary invention; indeed, "Rapunzel" is a prime example of this intermingling.

My retelling of "Rapunzel" takes its shape from both the Grimms' and earlier versions of the tale. I have tried to combine the most moving aspects of the story with the most satisfying structure, and to bring out its mysterious internal echoes. In selecting a setting, too, I considered the story's three countries of origin. The formal beauty of Italian Renaissance art seemed to fit well with a tale centered on the beauty of a young girl and a mother figure whose own youth is gone. Also, for me, the very image of a tower evokes the Italian landscape, where the campanile, or bell tower, plays a prominent role in architectural tradition. (The closeness of this word to *Campanula*, the name of the bellflower genus to which rapunzel belongs, helped me to believe I was setting out on the right track.)

As an interloper in the august tradition of Italian Renaissance painting, I have been humbled by my own attempts to achieve effects that any Renaissance painter's apprentice could have tossed off as though it were nothing: billowing drapery or the glint from a fingernail or light falling on tree leaves.

It would please me if my pictures served in some measure to spur an interest in the magnificent art from which I have drawn. My great hope, of course, is that this book may give pleasure to readers in and of itself.

PAUL O. ZELINSKY